Snow White and the Seven Dwarfs in

GRUMPY BIRTHDAY TO YOU!

WRITTEN BY **TRINA ROBBINS**

PENCILED BY **GONZALO MAYO**

INKED BY **STEVE GEORGE**

Pg. 51

101 DALMATIANS

LEASH FLAWS

WRITTEN BY **TRINA ROBBINS**

PENCILED BY **JOSÉ DELBO**

INKED BY **STEVE GEORGE**

Pg. 62

ACCLAIM BOOKS

275 SEVENTH AVE 14TH FL
NEW YORK, NY 10001
212 366 4900

PRESIDENT/PUBLISHER **FABIAN NICIEZA** • DIRECTOR OF BUSINESS AFFAIRS **HAYLEY EDEN**
AYR MARKETING DIRECTOR/PRODUCT MANAGER **STACY LOWE** • SENIOR EDITOR **EVAN SKOLNICK**
CIRCULATION MANAGER **LEE HANSEN** • MARKETING COORDINATORS **SCOTT MARTIN, STEPHEN VRATTOS**
PRODUCTION MANAGER/DESIGN DIRECTOR **SCOTT FRIEDLANDER** • MANUFACTURING MANAGER **ALANA ZDINAK**
OPERATIONS MANAGER **JAMES PERHAM** • SENIOR GRAPHIC DESIGNER **JOE CAPONSACCO**
GRAPHIC DESIGNERS **GINA DISKIN, RAY LEUNG, JADE MOEDE** • ART CORRECTIONIST **IRWIN BAUM**
AYR INTERNS **HARVEY RICHARDS III, SCOTT YOUNG**

Acclaim
young readers

P9-AFQ-580

"I WAS *SURPRISED* THAT I COULDN'T GET A RIDE WITH THE WARDROBE. SHE *ALWAYS* CARRIES ME AROUND IN ONE OF HER DRAWERS."

ruff

ruff

"I ONLY LOOKED AROUND FOR A *MINUTE*."

WOW! LOOK AT ALL THESE *BOOKS*.

ruff ruff ruff

"WE FOUND THE BALL. SO WE LEFT."

ruff

THAT'S THE WHOLE STORY. *HONEST*.

SO, IS THERE A *MASTER CRIMINAL* IN THE CASTLE?

MEG'S MISMATCHED MONOGRAMS

UH-OH-- I INVITED HERCULES' RELATIVES-- THE SEVEN GREAT GODDESSES-- TO LUNCH...

...BUT I'VE MIXED UP THEIR PLACE CARDS AND TITLE STICKERS!

HELP MEG... MATCH EACH GODDESS WITH HER OFFICIAL POSITION ON MOUNT OLYMPUS!

1. ATHENA

A. GODDESS OF THE HUNT

2. HERA

B. GODDESS OF WISDOM & THE ARTS

3. HESTIA

C. GODDESS OF THE RAINBOW

4. APHRODITE ♥

D. GODDESS OF YOUTH

5. IRIS

E. GODDESS OF HOME & HEARTH

6. HEBE

F. QUEEN OF THE GODS

7. ARTEMIS

G. GODDESS OF LOVE & BEAUTY

IT'S A SMELL FROM WHEN I WAS *YOUNG!*

Waaaaahhhh!

YOU?!!

YOUNG?!

hehehee

hahahaha!

WE WERE *ALL* YOUNG ONCE. EVEN THIS OLD *CATHEDRAL.*

THAT'S IT! IT SMELLS LIKE THOSE PINK ROSES THAT USED TO GROW ALL OVER THE CITY, BEFORE IT GOT SO *BUILT UP.*

I HAVEN'T SMELLED IT IN *YEARS.* I FEEL SO HAPPY I JUST WANT TO ⸬SNIFF⸬ ⸬SNIFF⸬

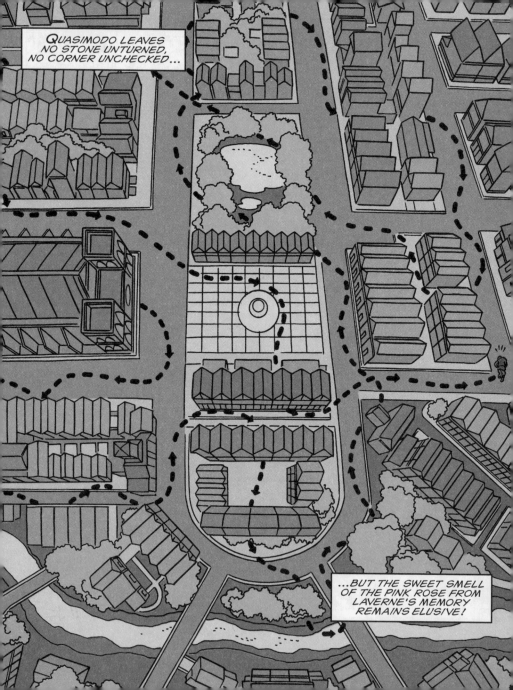

SAVE $10.00 ON

ENCHANTMENT!

SAVE $10.00 OFF THE RETAIL PRICE WHEN YOU SUBSCRIBE TO DISNEY'S ENCHANTING STORIES! THAT'S LIKE GETTING TWO ISSUES FREE!

EACH ENCHANTING STORYBOOK FEATURES 64 FULL-COLOR PAGES OF YOUR FAVORITE DISNEY CHARACTERS IN ALL-NEW FUN-FILLED ADVENTURES! ENJOY HOURS OF READING FUN WITH YOUR FRIENDS FROM BEAUTY AND THE BEAST, POCAHONTAS, SNOW WHITE AND THE SEVEN DWARFS, HERCULES, 101 DALMATIANS, AND THE HUNCHBACK OF NOTRE DAME!

YES! PLEASE SEND ME 6 ISSUES OF DISNEY'S ENCHANTING STORIES FOR ONLY $17.00.
I UNDERSTAND THAT I'LL SAVE A TOTAL OF $10.00 OFF THE COVER PRICE!
(PLEASE PRINT)

NAME _____

ADDRESS _____

CITY _____

STATE _____ ZIP _____

SEND A CHECK OR MONEY ORDER PAYABLE TO

ACCLAIM BOOKS

(NY RESIDENTS, PLEASE ADD APPLICABLE SALES TAX.)
PHOTOCOPIES OF THIS FORM ARE ACCEPTABLE.
SORRY - NOT AVAILABLE TO RESIDENTS OF CANADA.

SEND TO:
ACCLAIM BOOKS
YOUNG READER
SUBSCRIPTIONS
PO BOX 40
VERNON, NJ 07462

OR CALL 1-888-9-ACCLAIM!

OFFER EXPIRES 11/30/97

© Disney

KEY CODE 02K

WELL, THAT'S GOOD, BECAUSE I'D LIKE YOU TO COME *FISHING* WITH ME.

FISHING? OH, THAT SOUNDS LIKE FUN! I WOULD LOVE TO GO.

LET'S *HURRY!* I SAW A GREAT BIG *TROUT*, AND I DON'T WANT ANYONE *ELSE* TO GET HIM!

SNIFF SNIFF

SNIFF SNIFF

CRUK

BOINGGGG

SKAAAANGGG

POING

SLING

FWWWOOOM

LATER...

THAT'S MEEKO--HE'S IN TROUBLE!

SQUEAK SQUEAK

BANG

OH, MEEKO!

THAT'S MY FATHER'S BASKET! HOW *COULD* YOU?

(50)

HO, HO! POCAHONTAS' LITTLE FRIEND RUNS LIKE THE *DEER!*

HE RUNS LIKE THERE IS *TROUBLE.*

CHILD! WHAT IS *WRONG*?

N-NOTHING, FATHER.

YOU ARE NOT *CRYING* LIKE THIS BECAUSE *NOTHING* IS WRONG--PLEASE TELL ME.

IT...IT...WAS A *PRESENT* FOR YOU, AND NOW IT IS *RUINED.*

AHHH, THE *RACCOON.*

YES.

The End

53